Dog Portraits
Coloring Book

ADULT COLORING BOOK FEATURING
DOG FACE DESIGNS OF TOP DOG BREEDS
FOR STRESS RELIEF COLORING

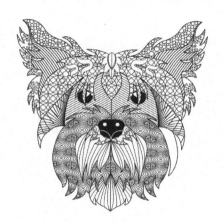

GINA TROWLER

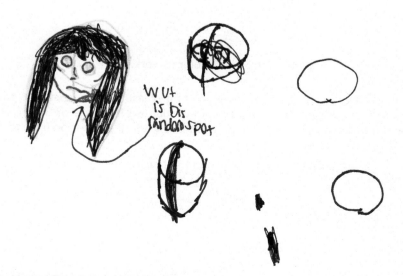

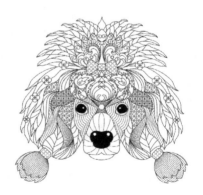

ISBN-13: 978-1530549092 | ISBN-10: 1530549094

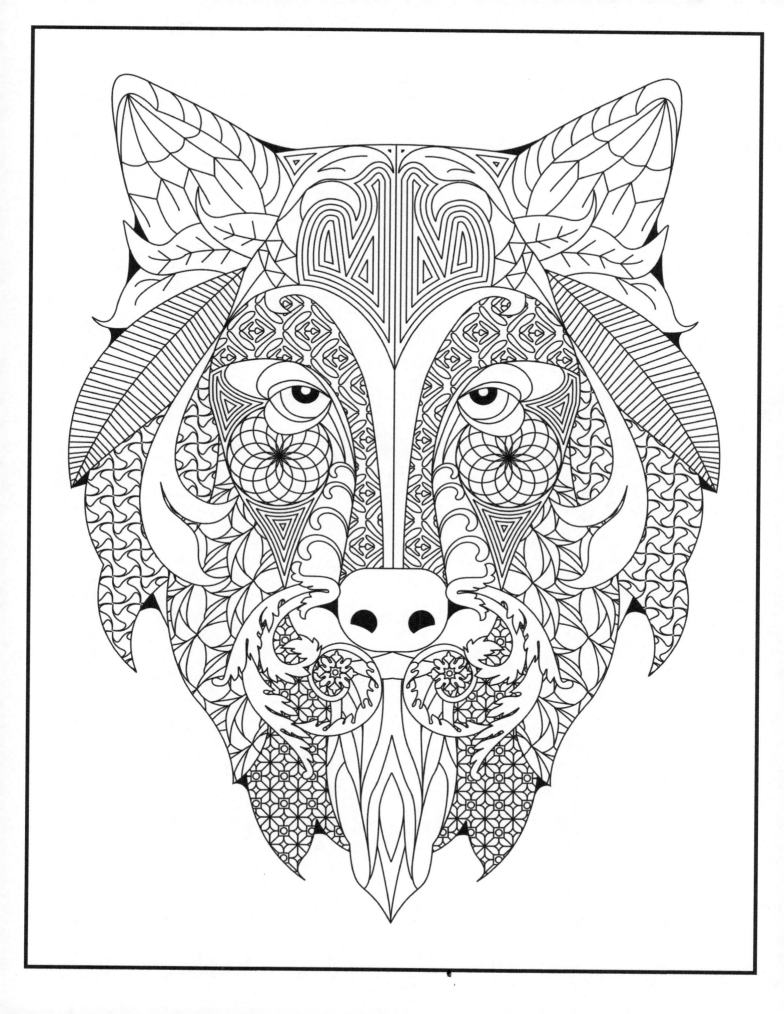

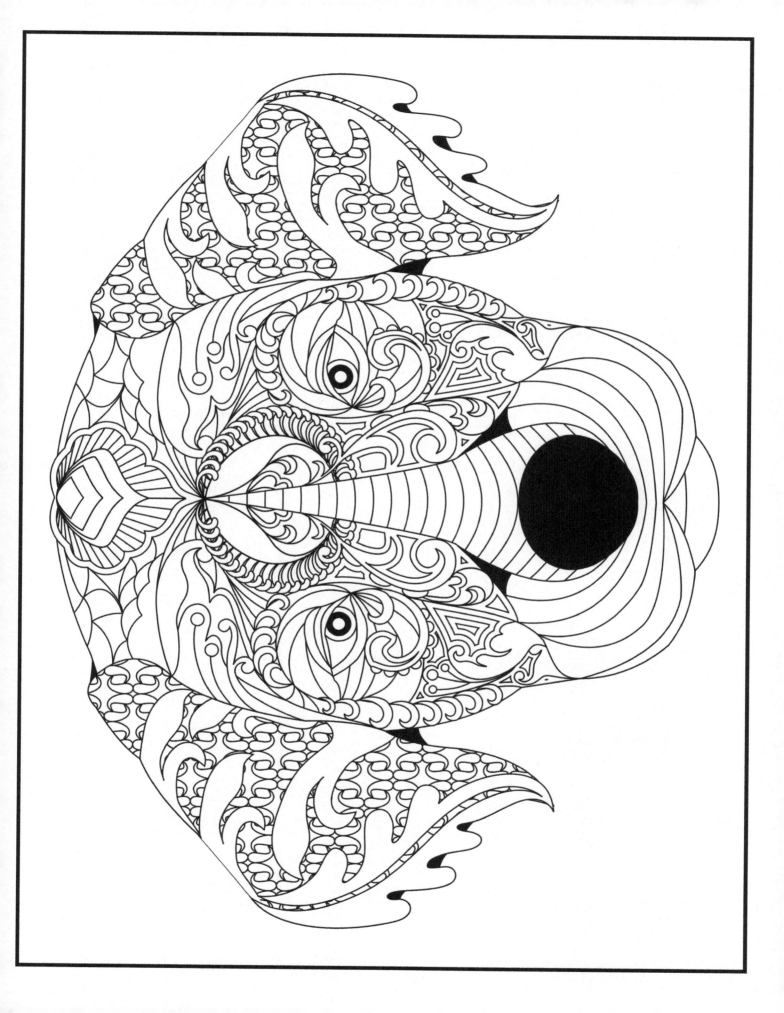

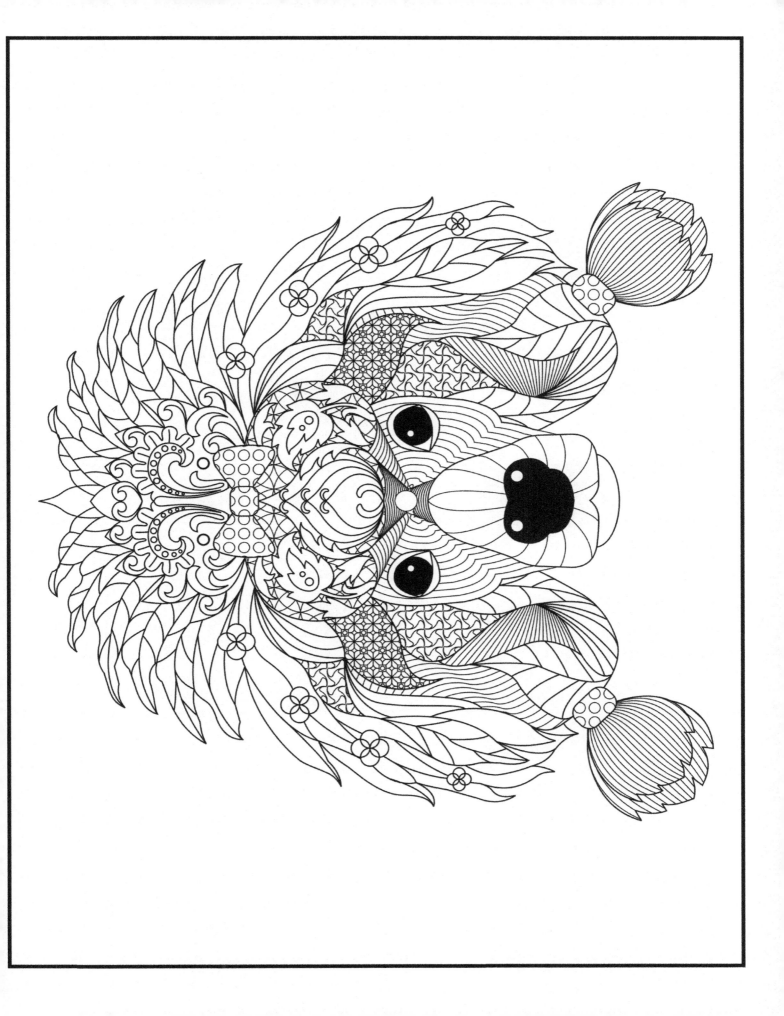

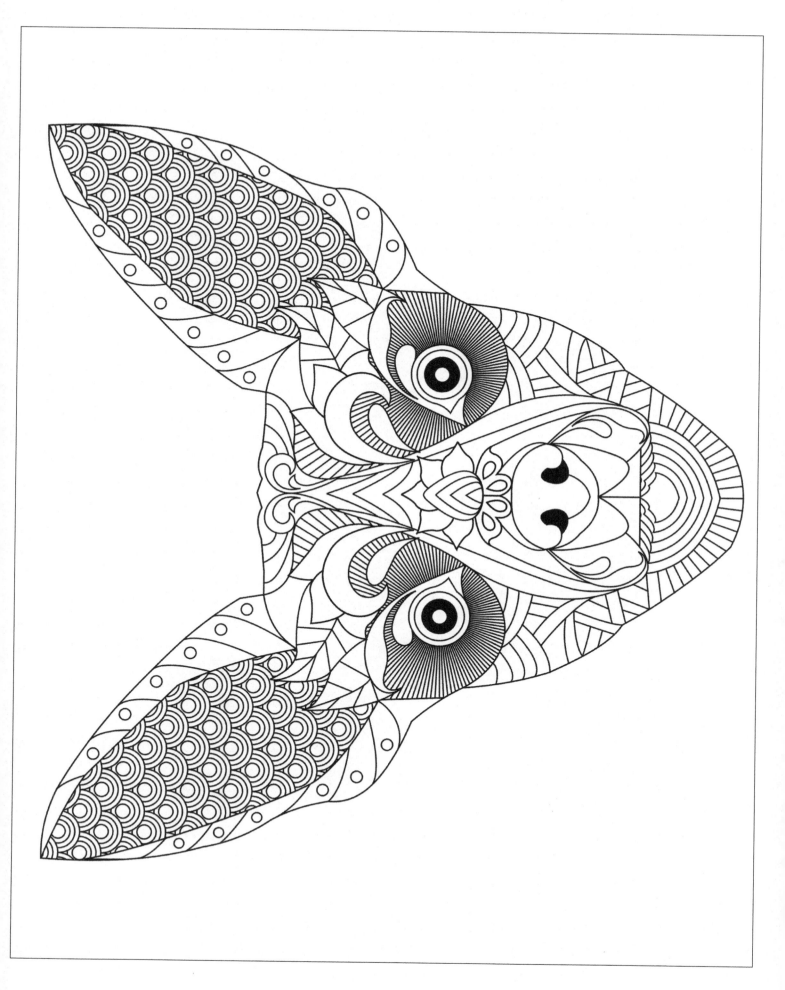

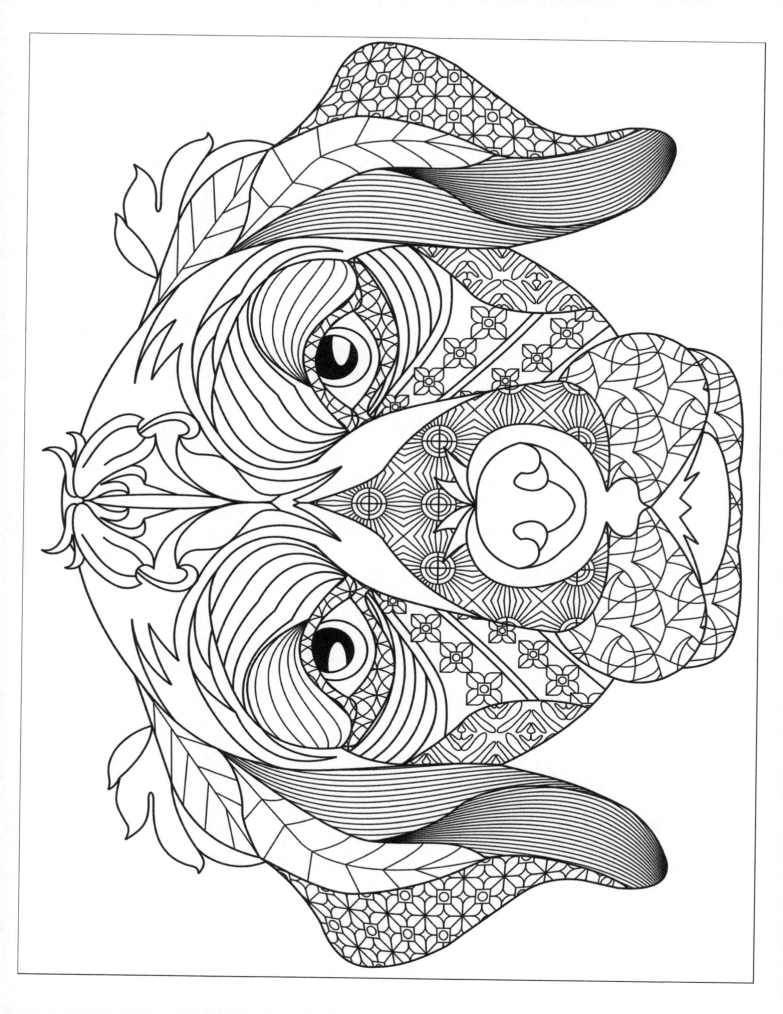

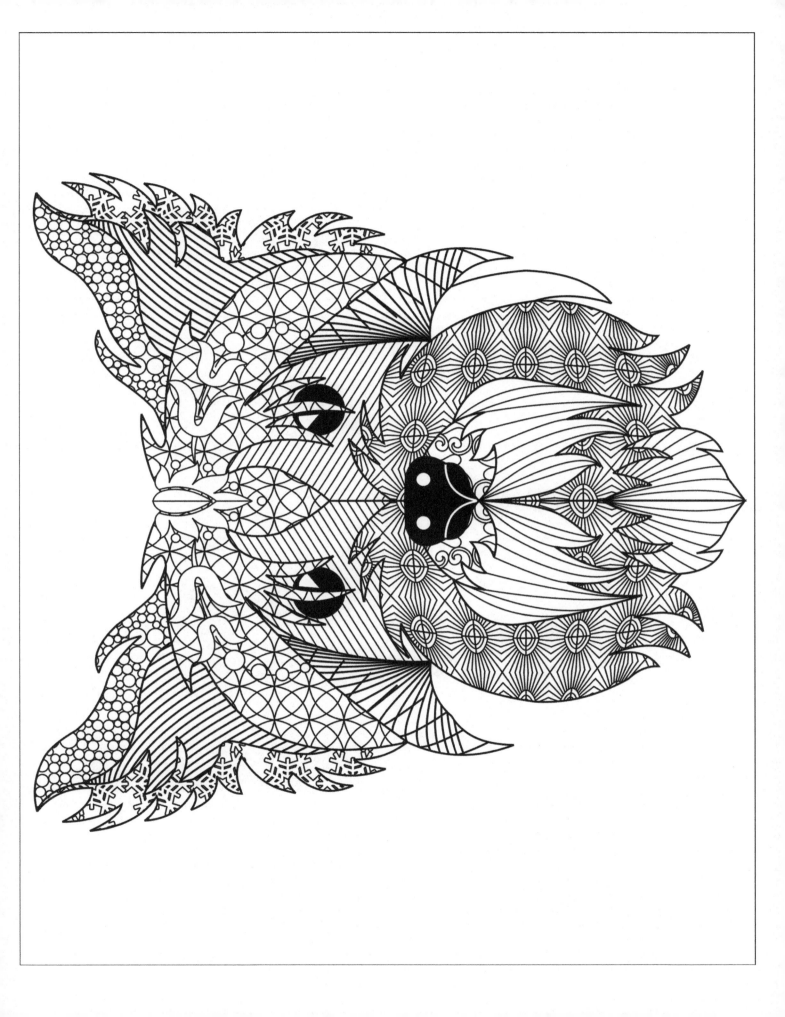

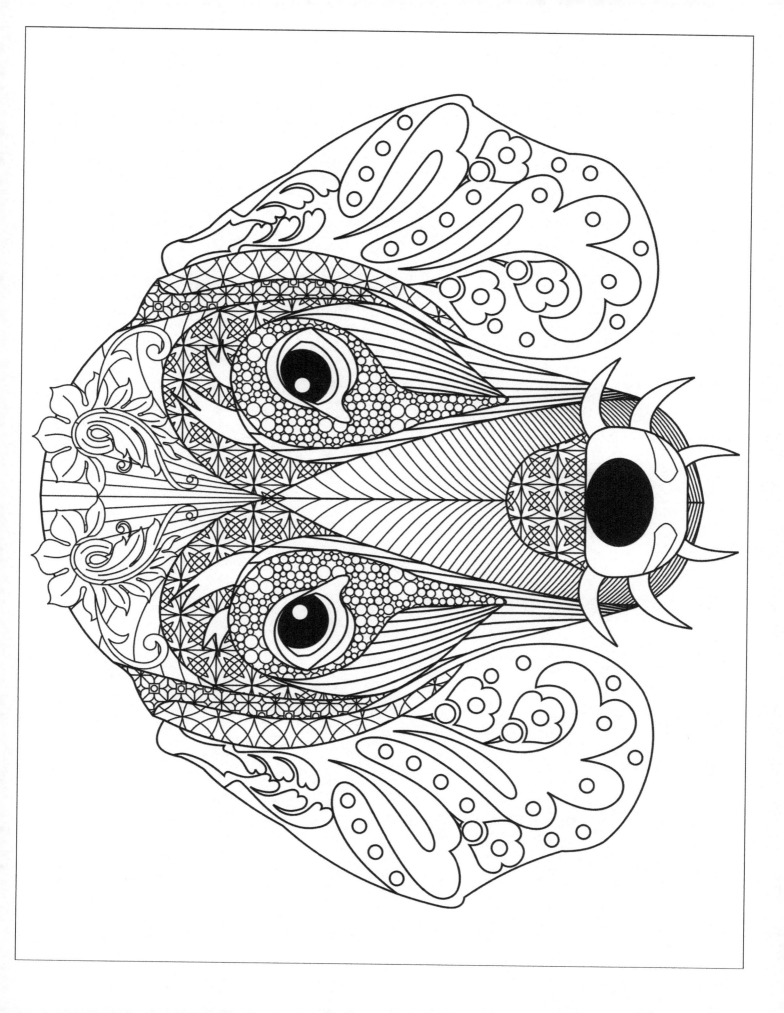

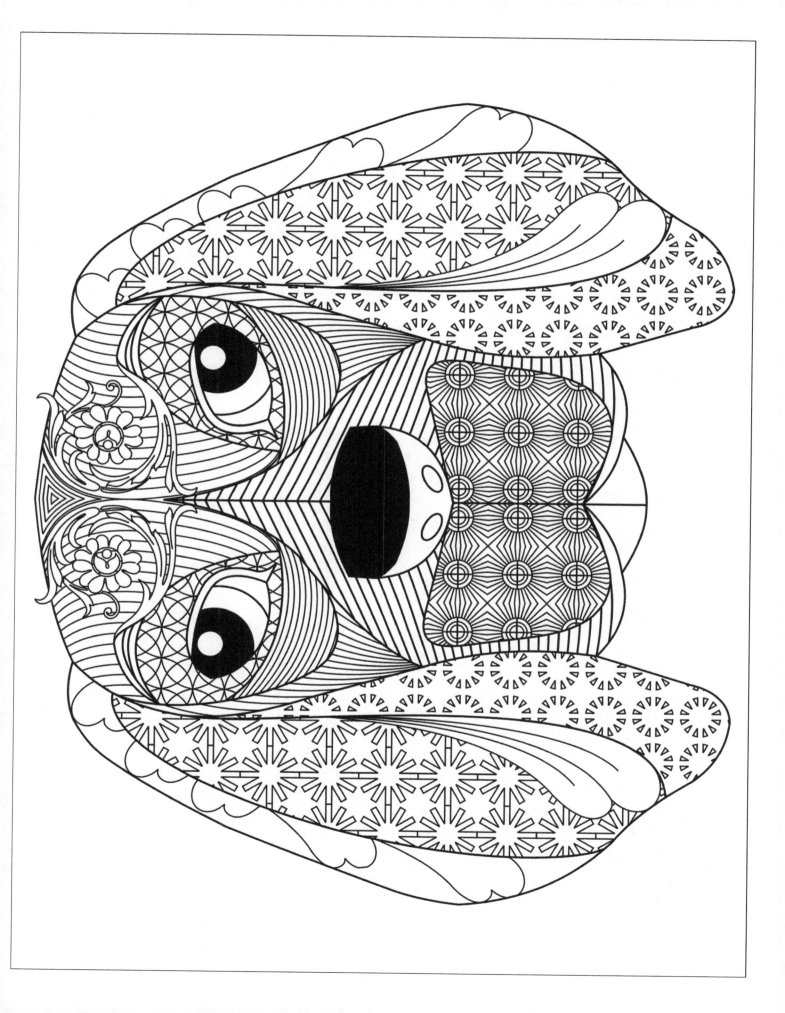

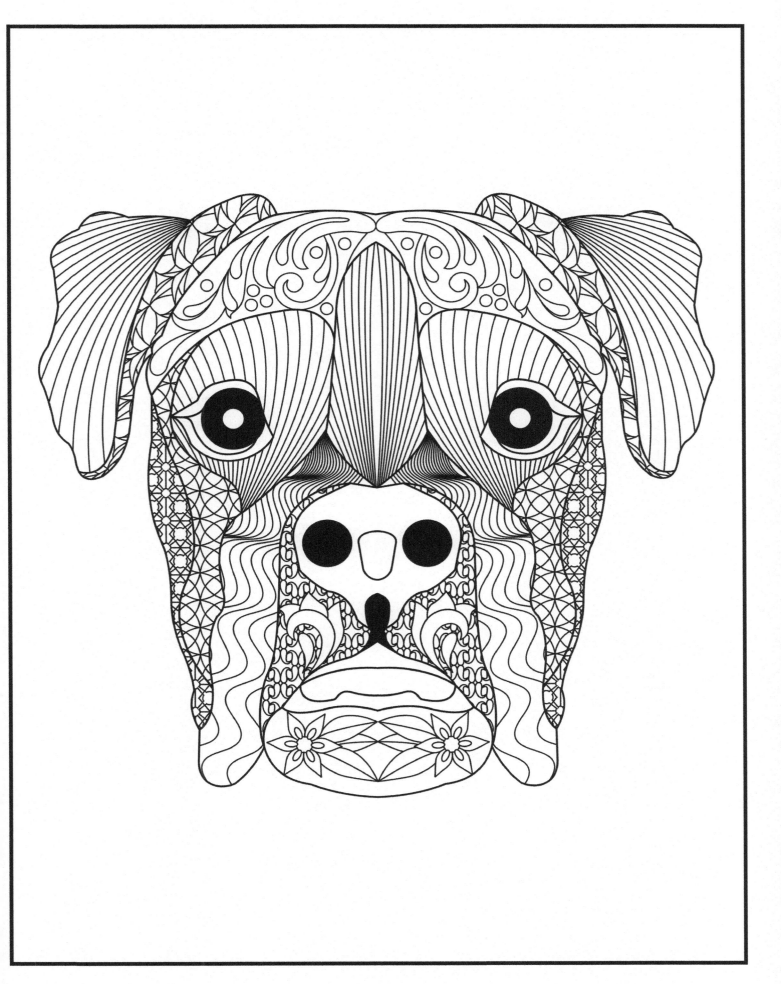

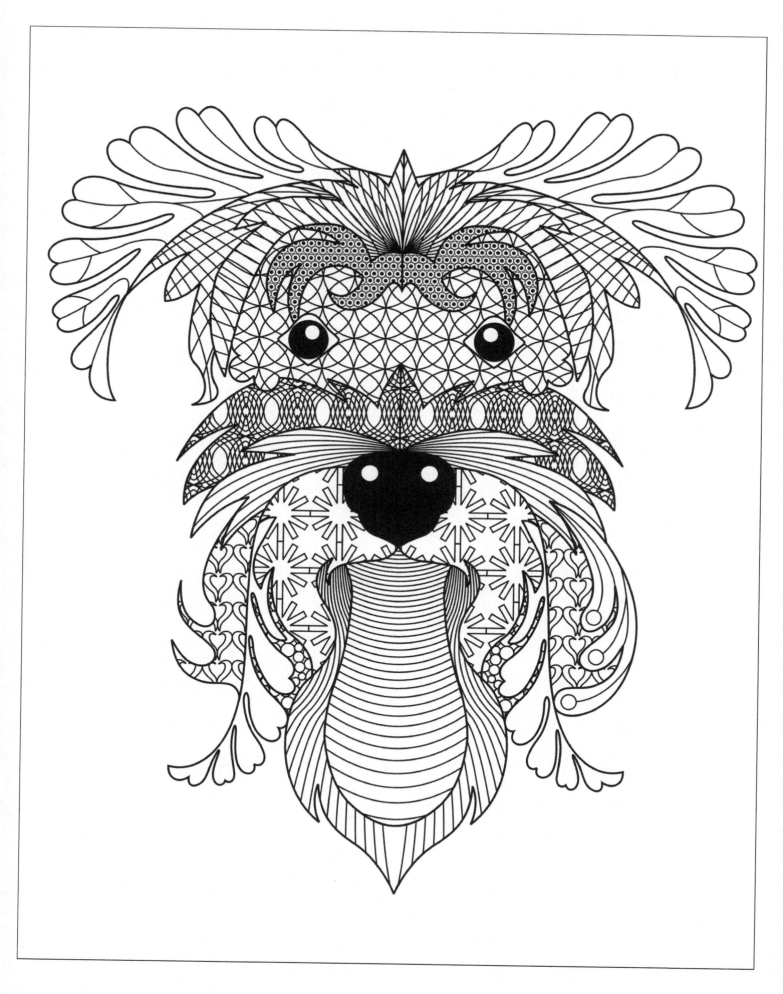

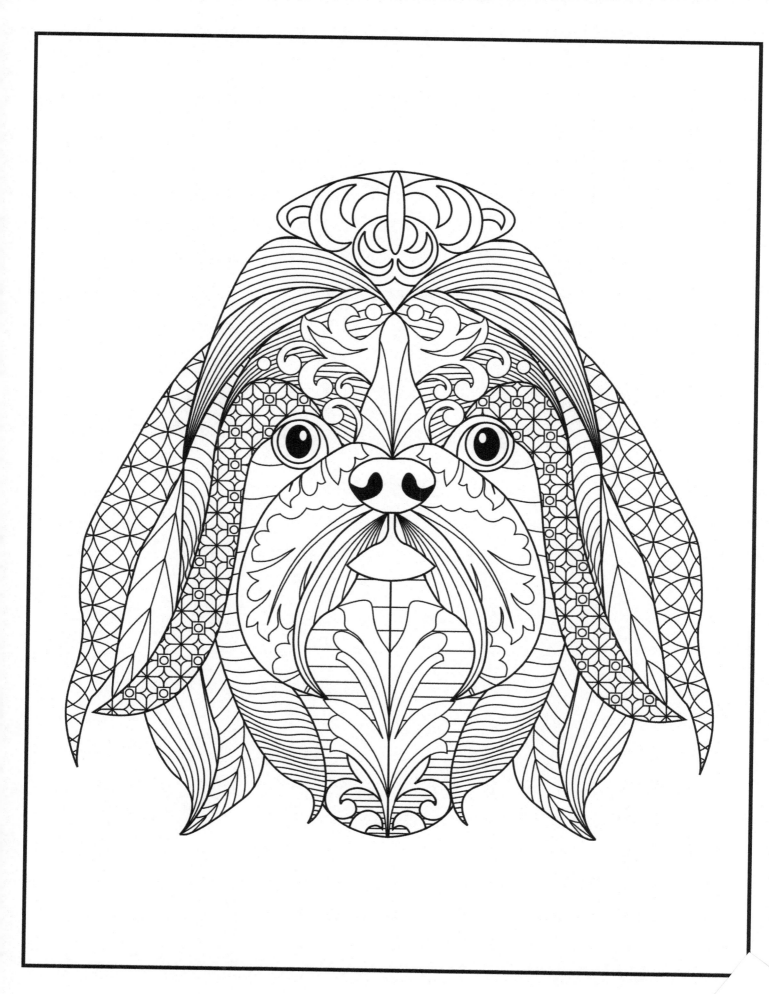

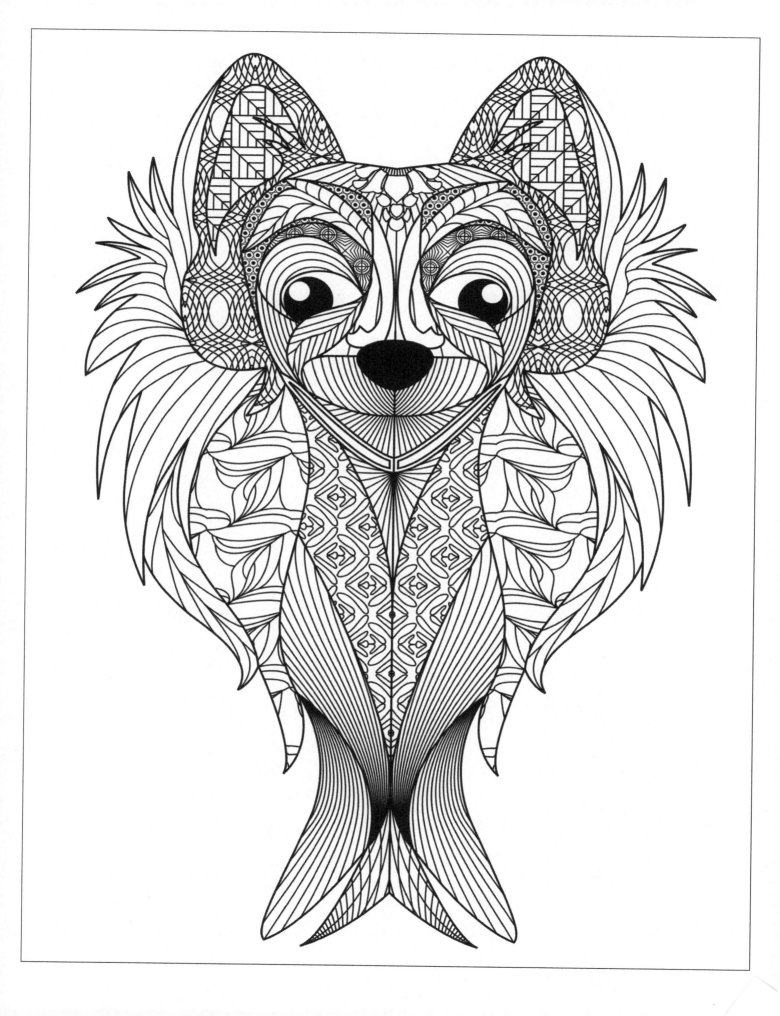

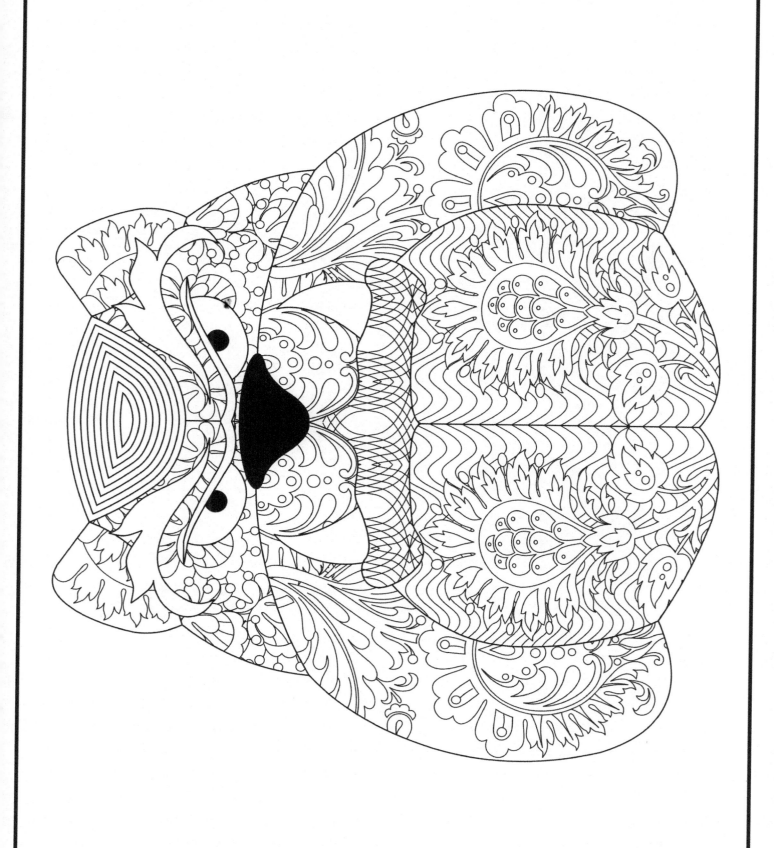

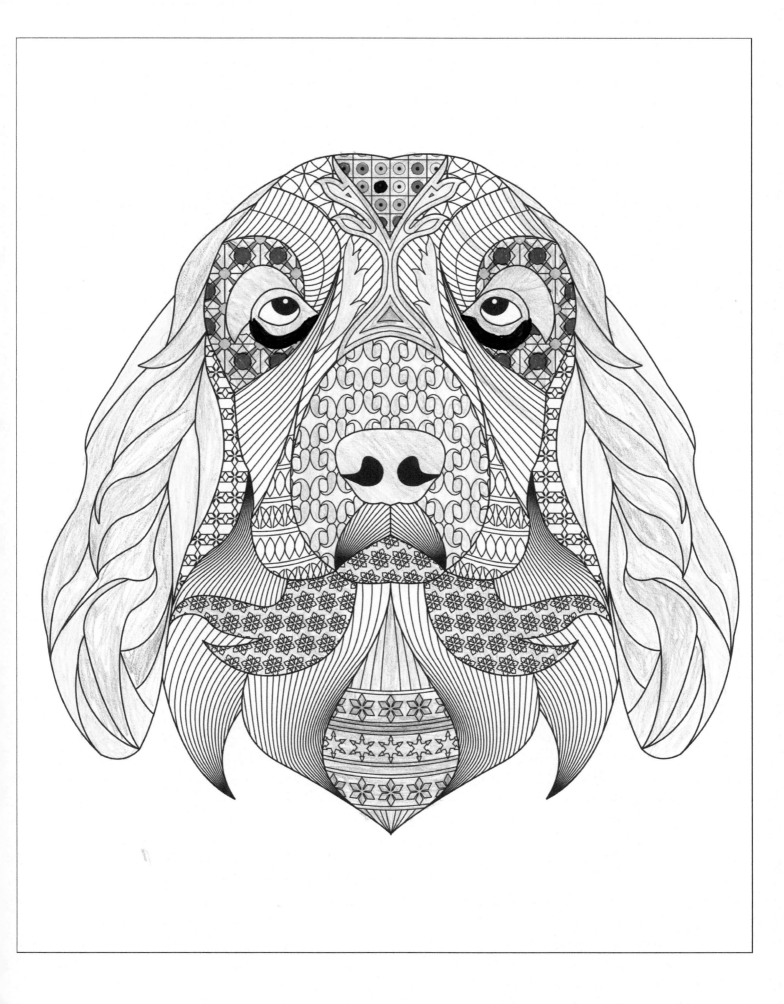

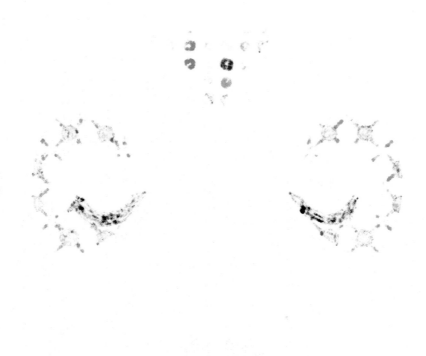

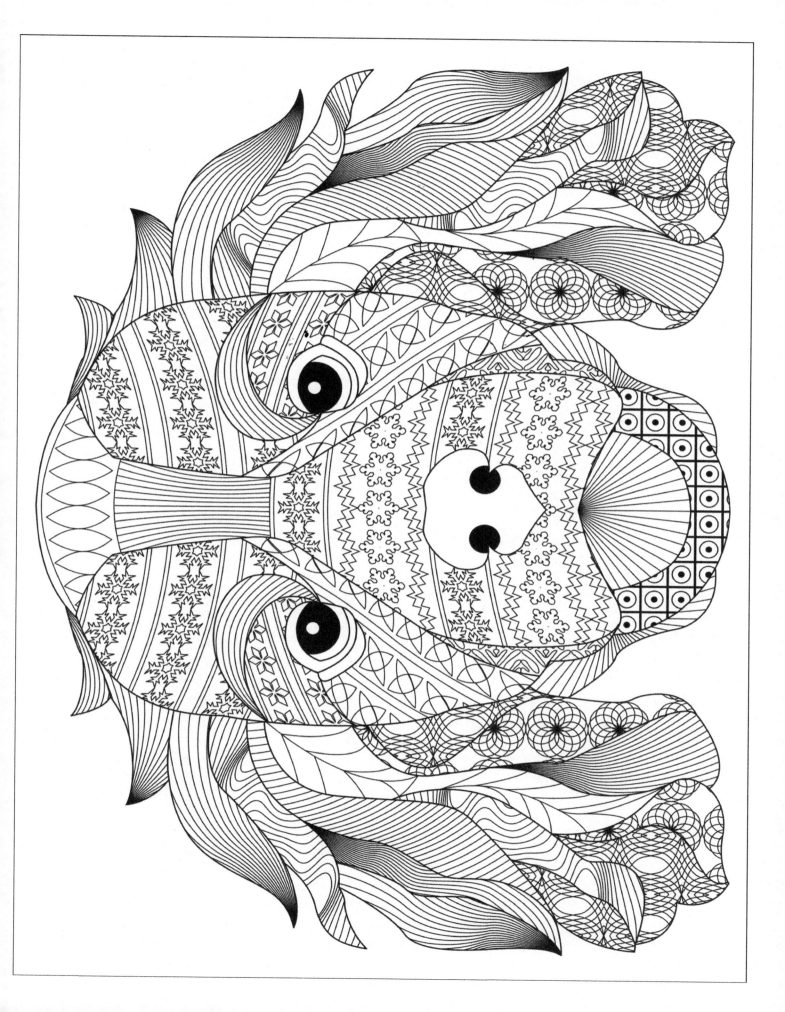

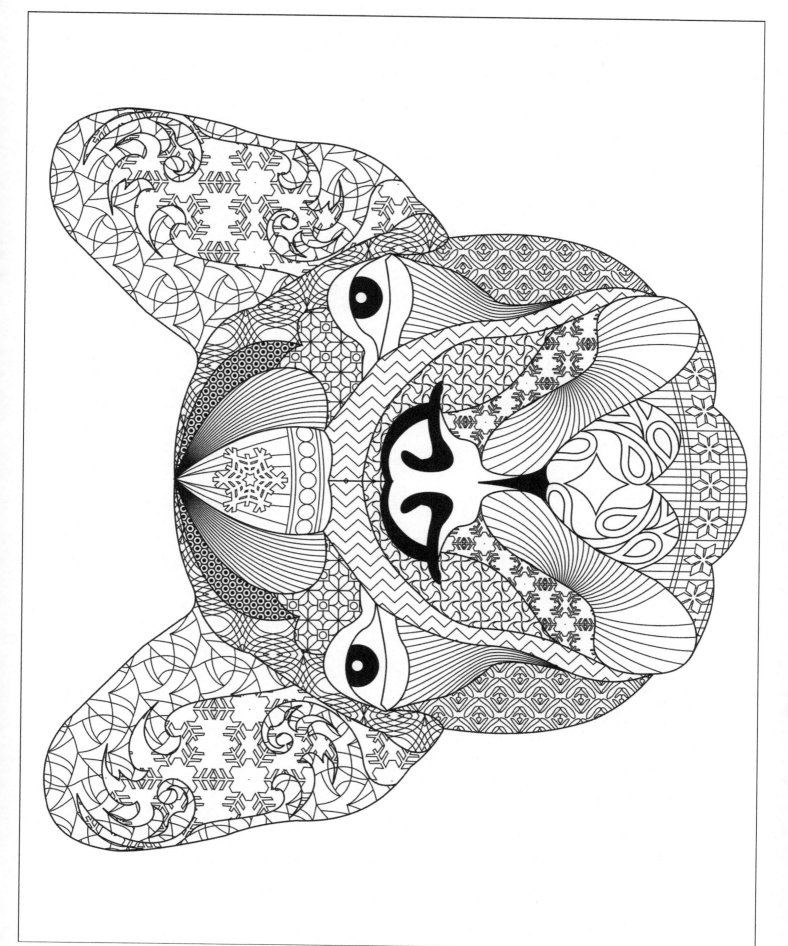

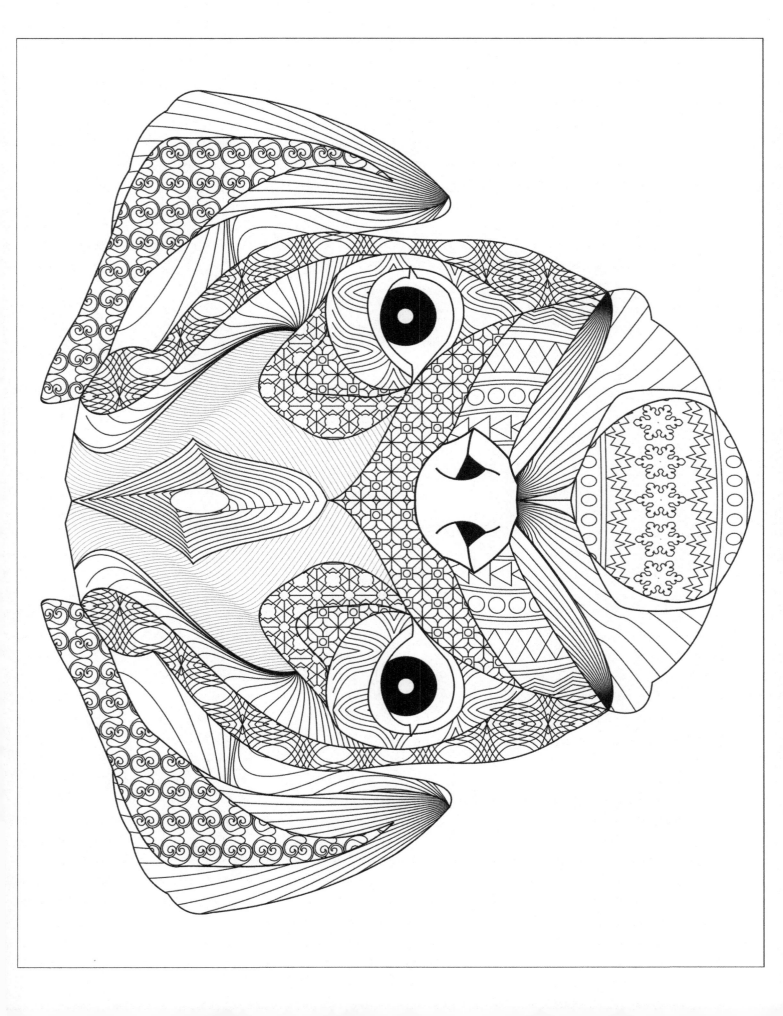

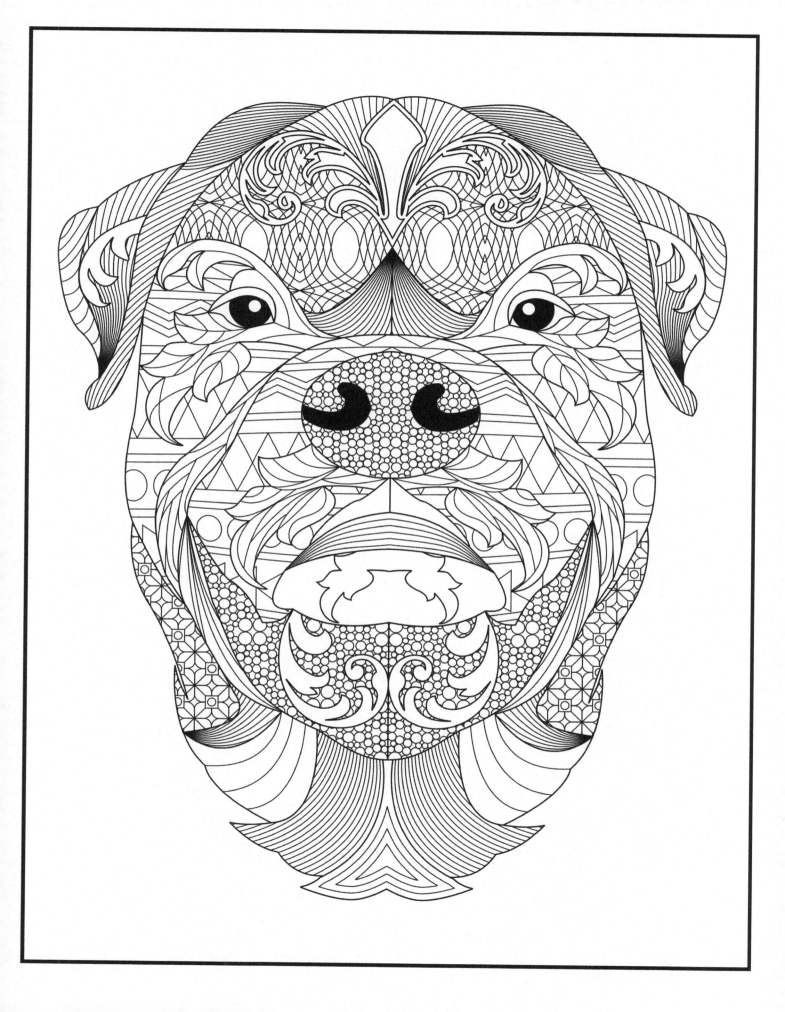

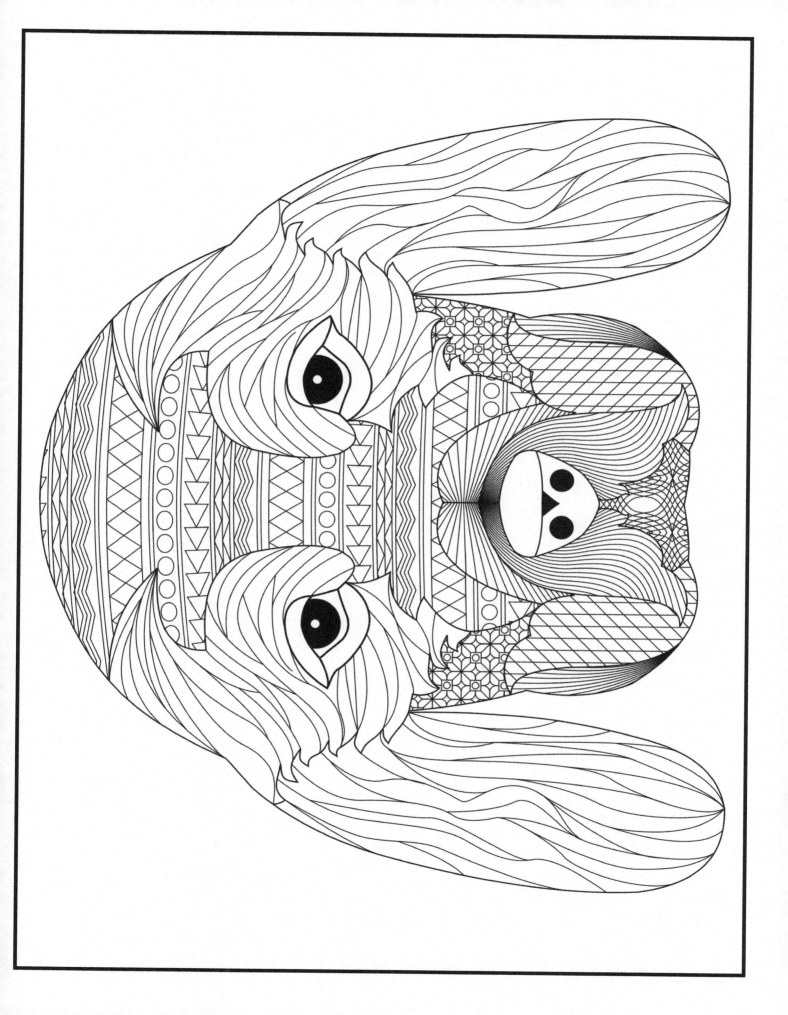

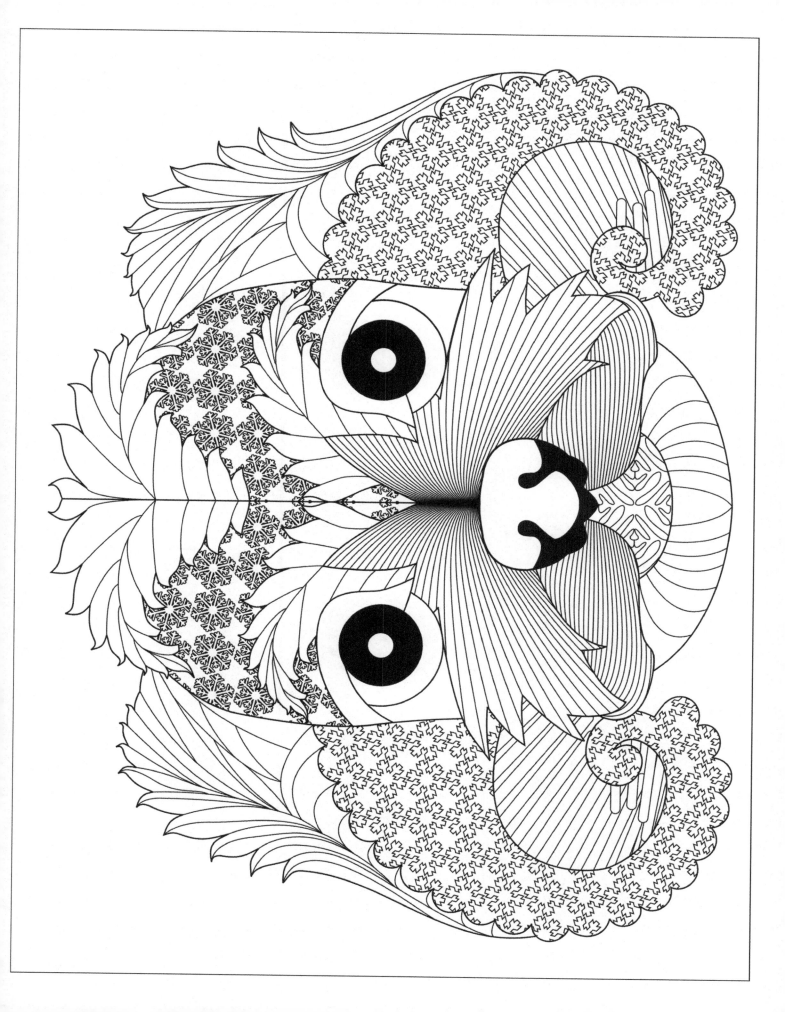

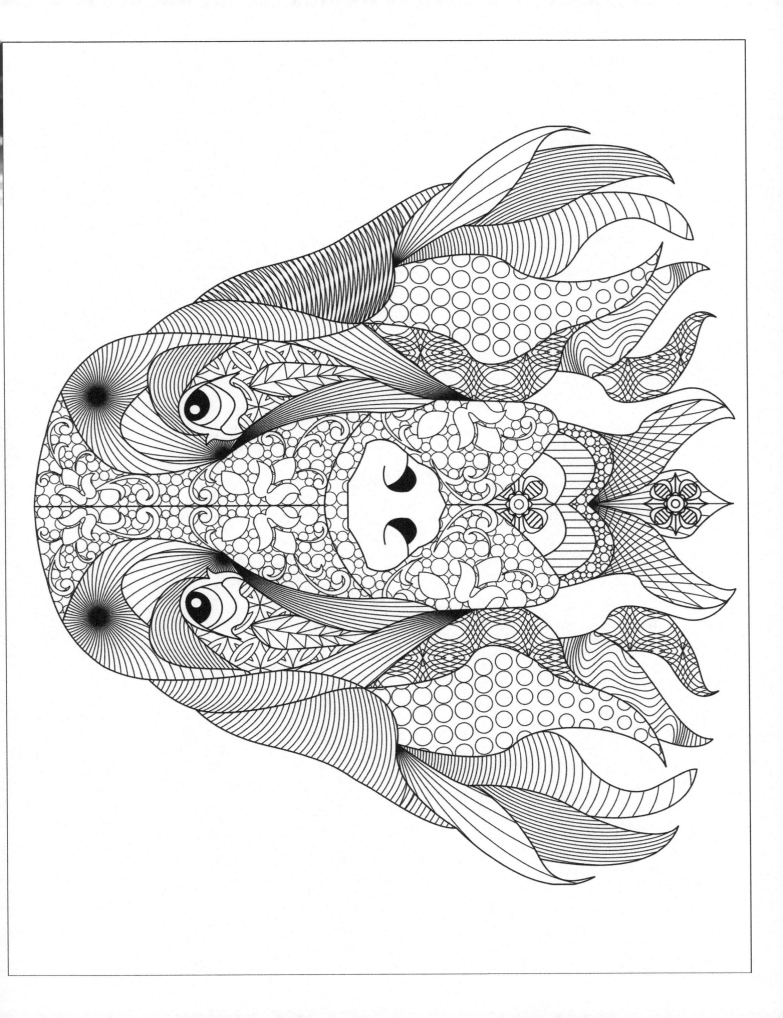

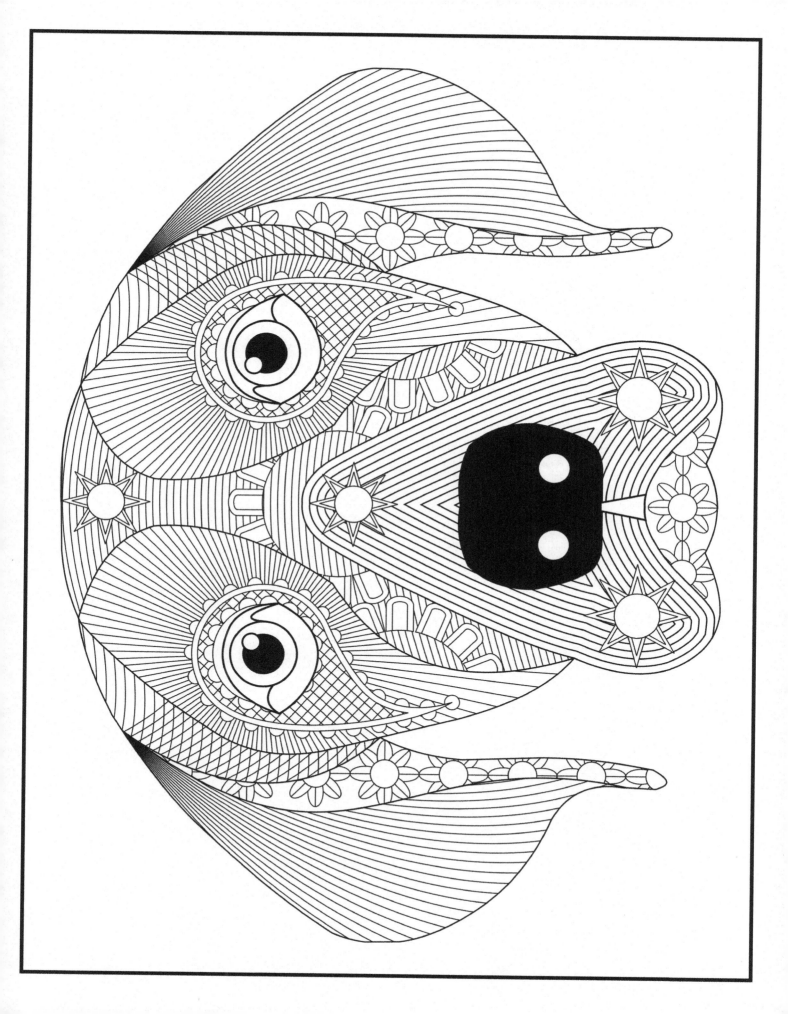

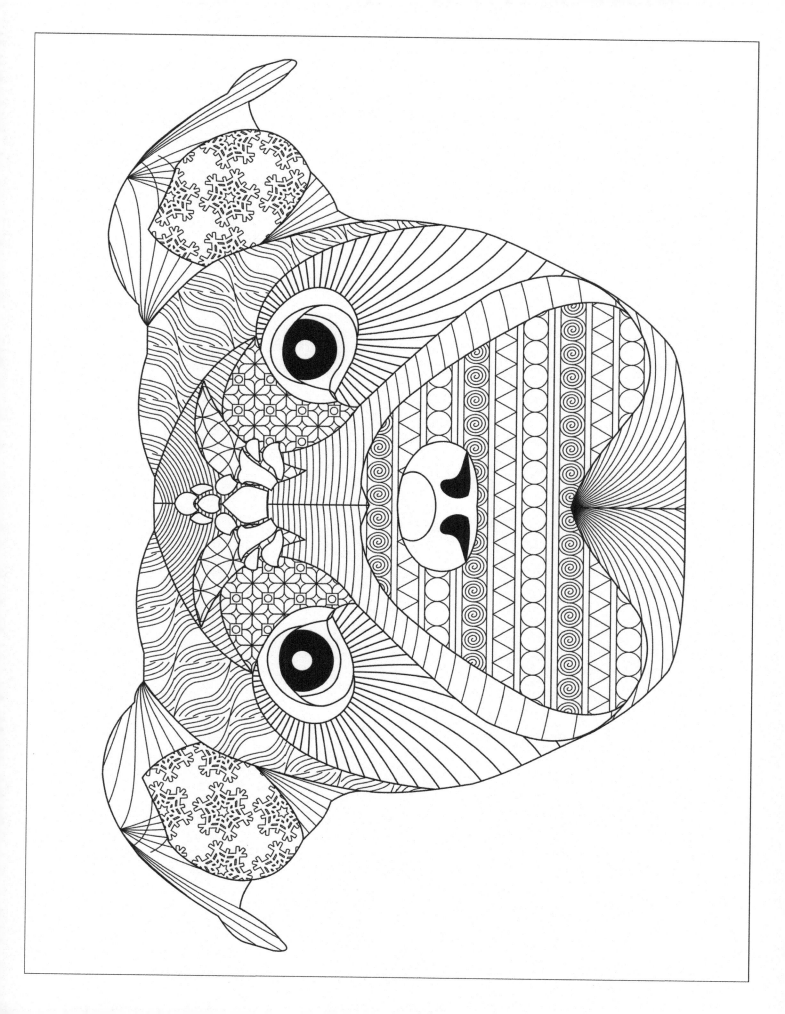

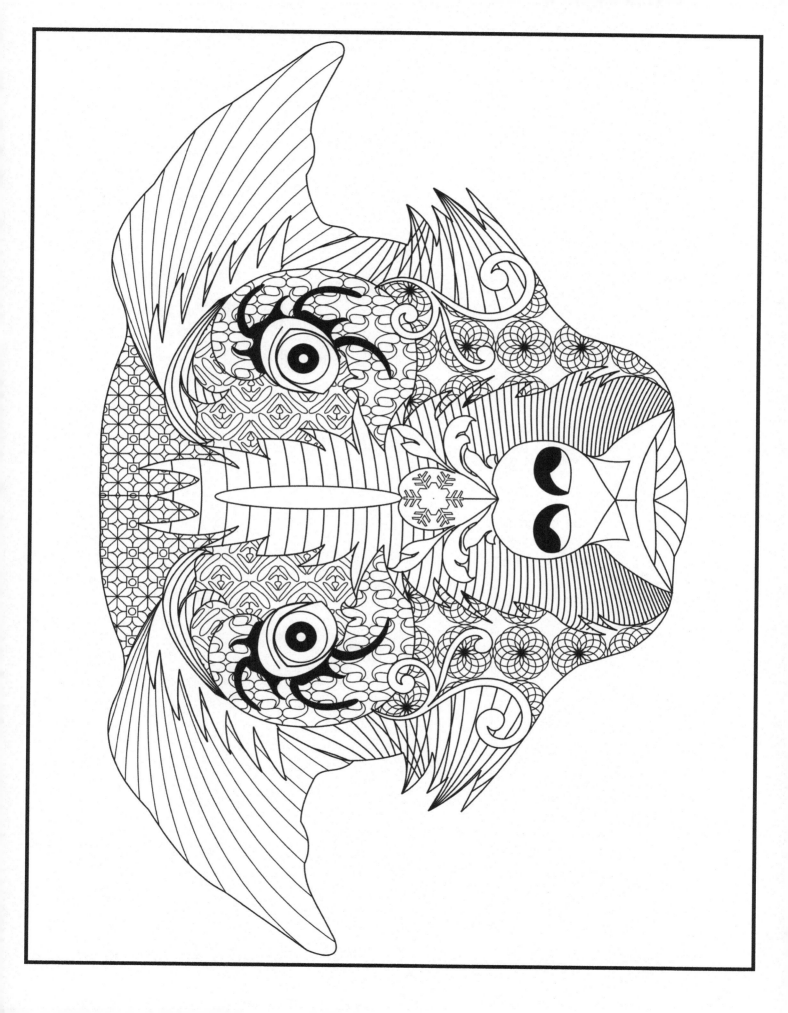

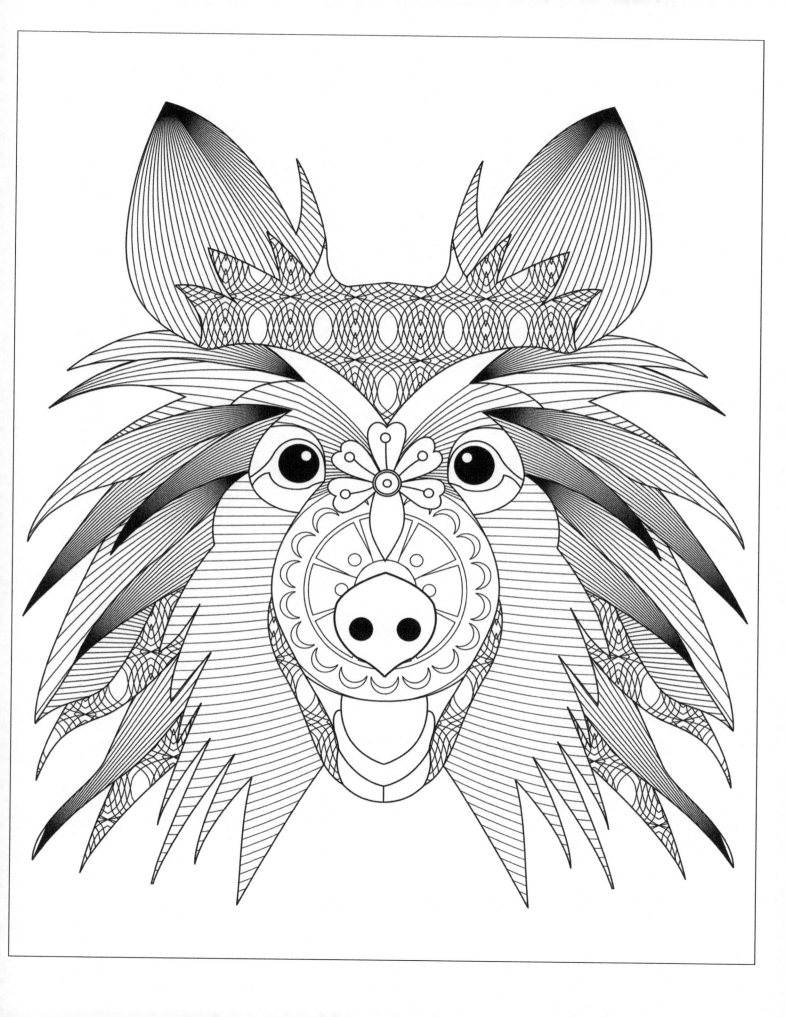

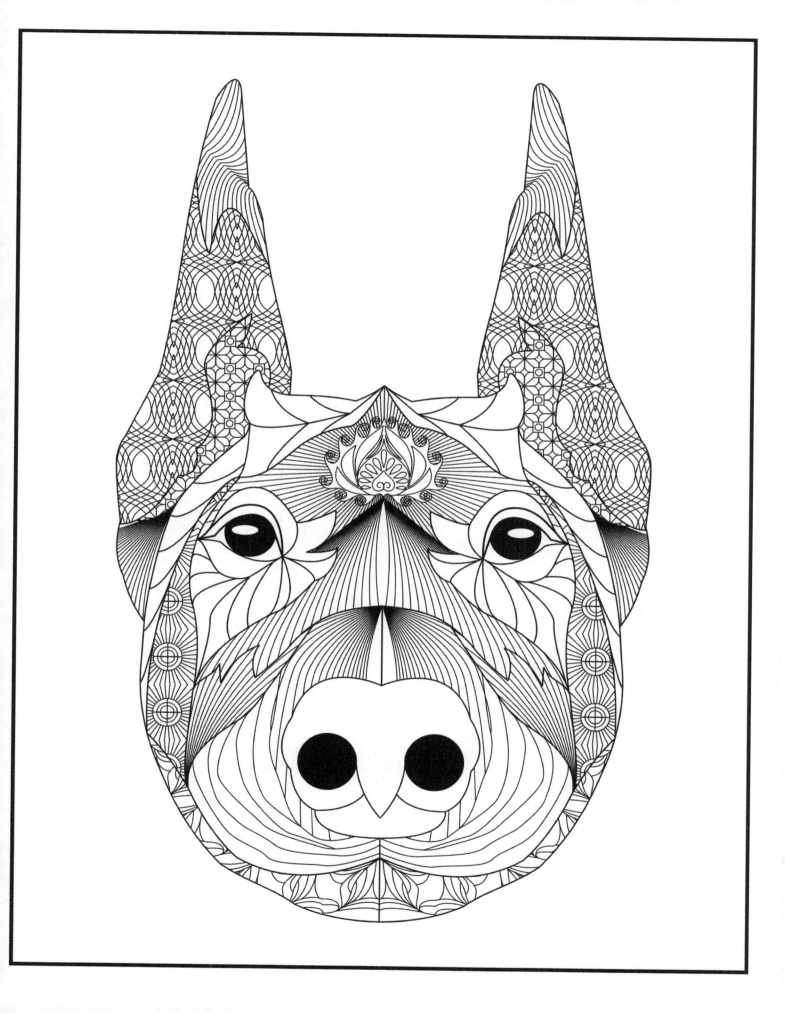

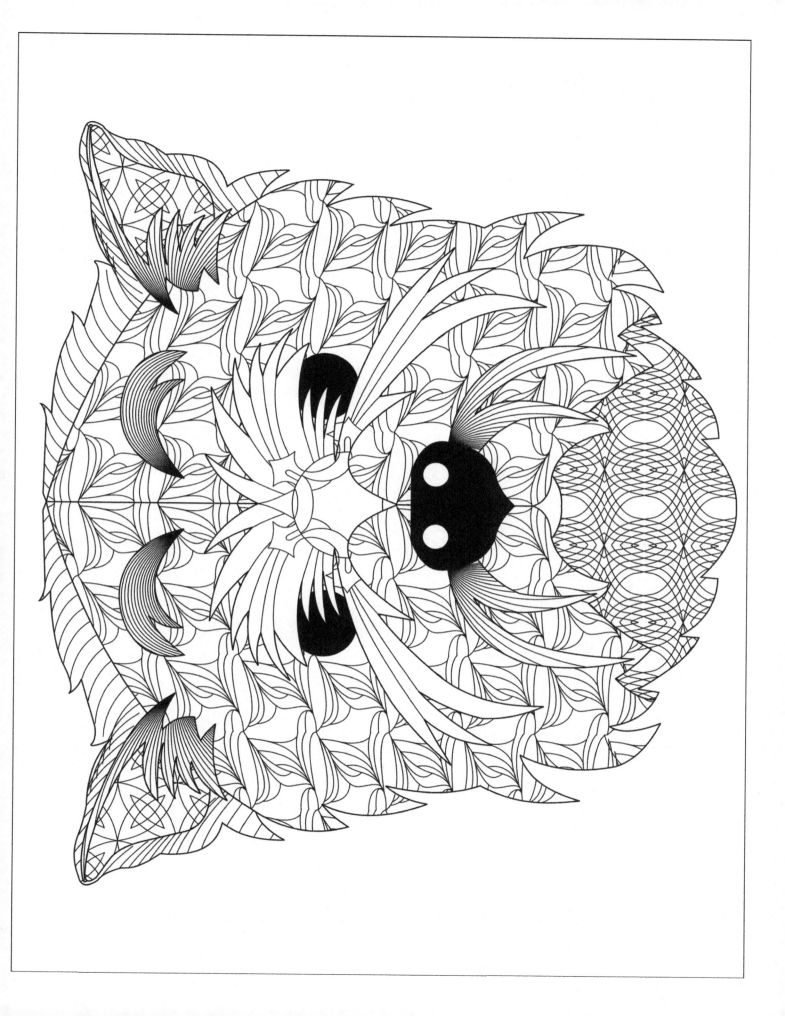

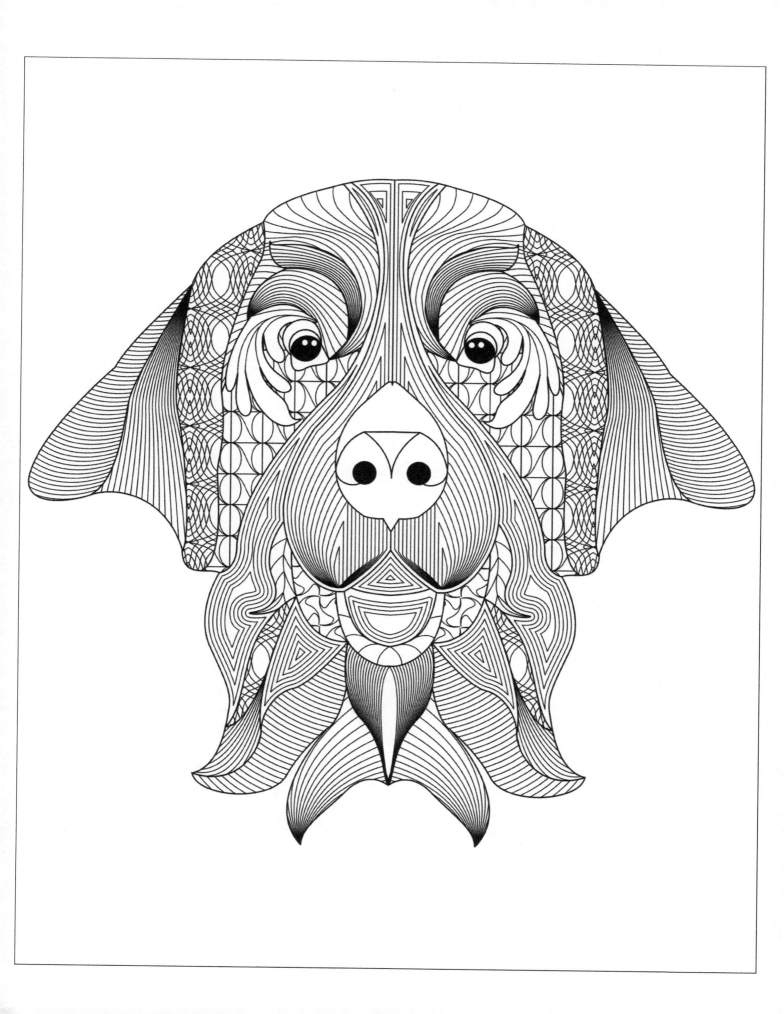

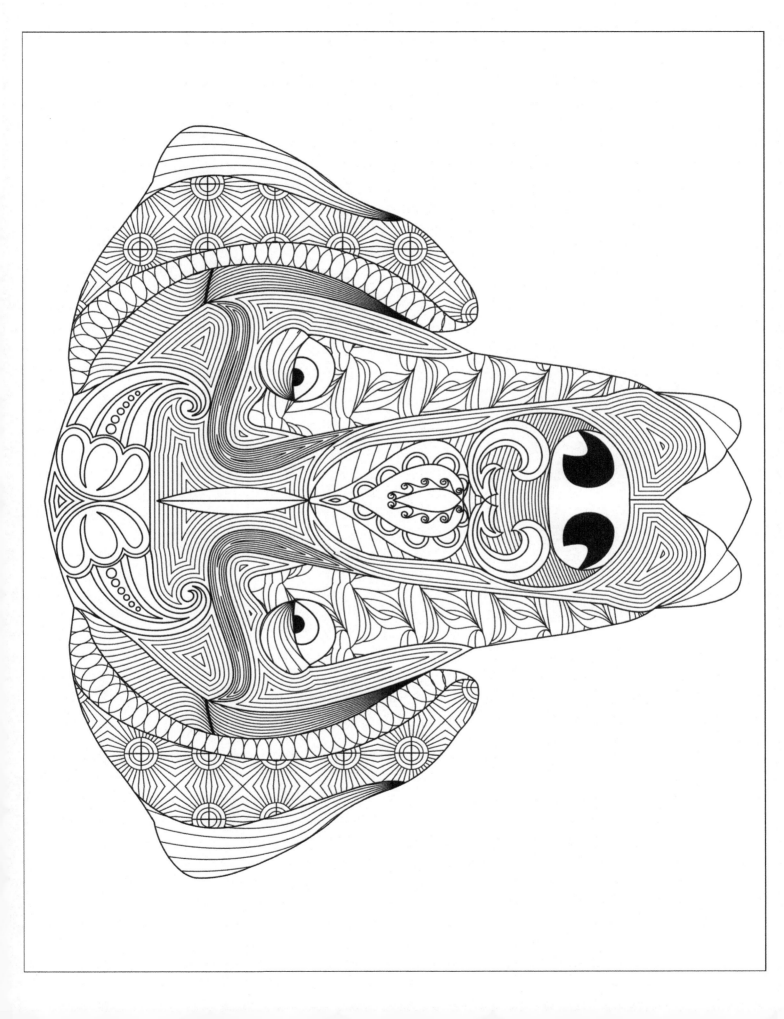

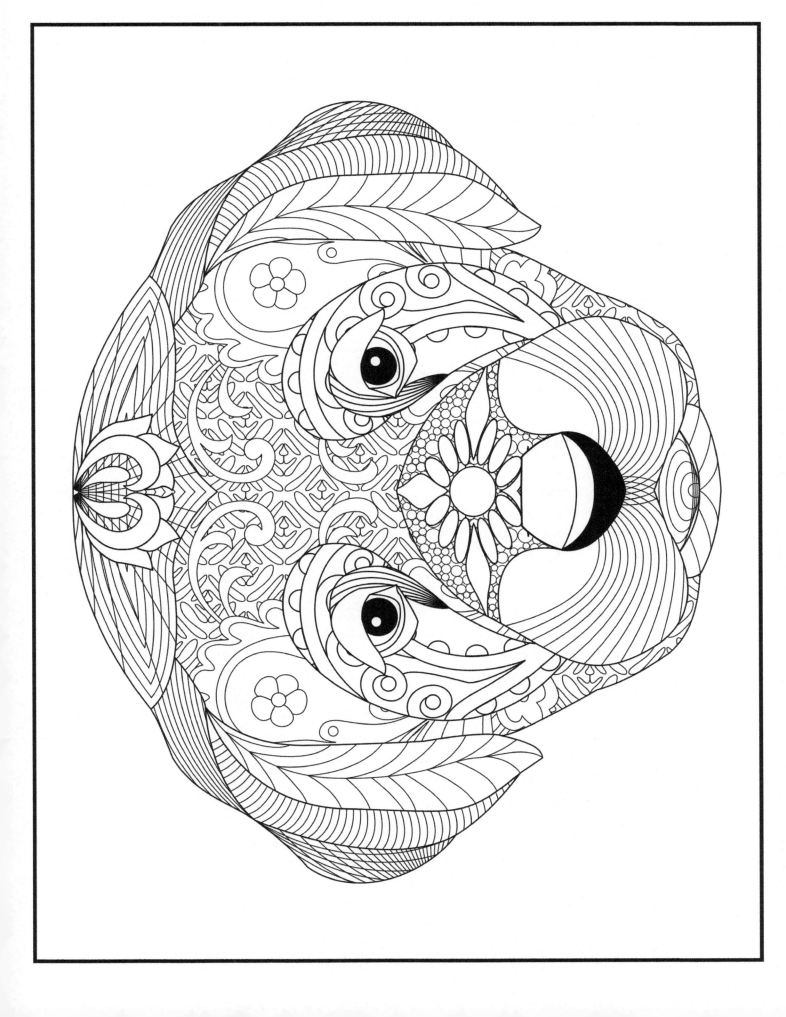

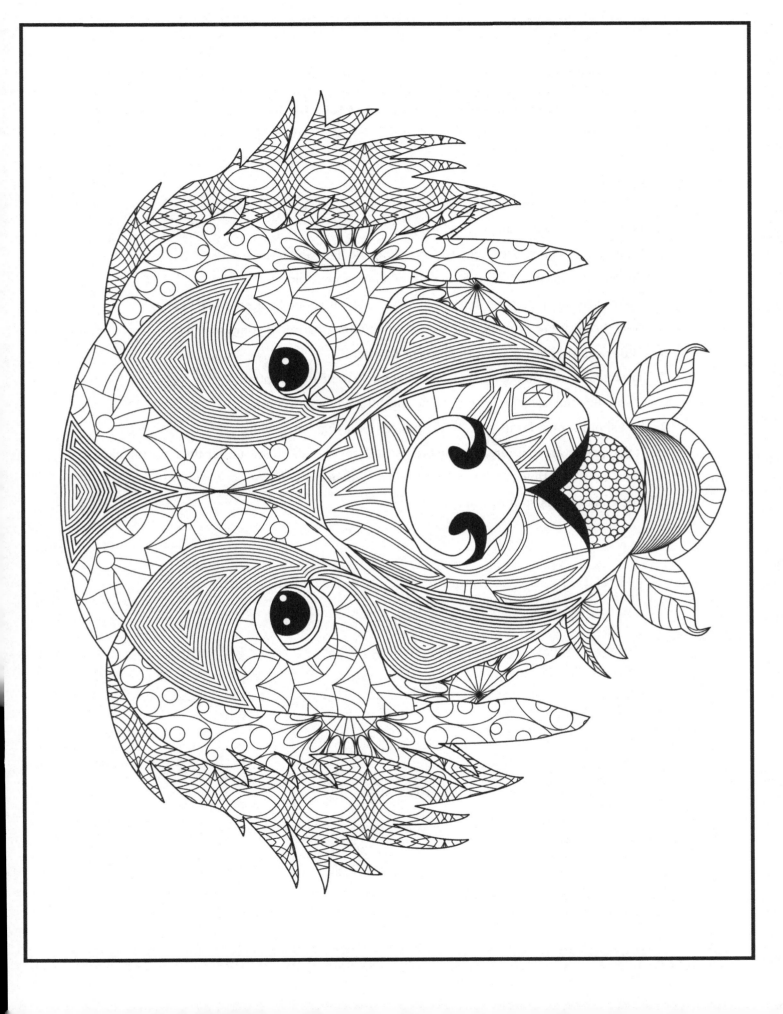

COLORING GUIDE

1. Find a quiet place to do your coloring.
2. Choose your colors according to your liking. Be light and open-minded.
3. Choose to color in bright natural light whenever possible.
4. Make sure you are sitting in a comfortable seat with good back support. Relax.
5. Don't be afraid to express your creativity and imagination in your coloring.
6. Choose your favorite artwork patterns to color.
7. Try to color at a time when you are least likely to be interrupted.
8. If you like music, listen to something soothing while you color.
9. You should consider using coloring pencils over regular crayons.
10. If you prefer art markers, it is best to use a sheet of craft plastic under the coloring page.
11. Take your own time coloring - stop coloring whenever you like.
12. The end result is your own masterpiece.

IMPORTANT:

In order to prevent color-bleeding no image was placed on the opposite side of each artwork printed.

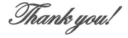

Made in the USA
Columbia, SC
17 April 2020